Musical Max

by **Robert Kraus**
pictures by **Jose Aruego & Ariane Dewey**

SIMON & SCHUSTER BOOKS FOR YOUNG READERS

Published by Simon & Schuster
New York · London · Toronto · Sydney · Tokyo · Singapore

SIMON & SCHUSTER BOOKS FOR YOUNG READERS

Simon & Schuster Building, Rockefeller Center, 1230 Avenue of the Americas, New York, New York 10020

SIMON & SCHUSTER BOOKS FOR YOUNG READERS is a trademark of Simon & Schuster.

Designed by Lucille Chomowicz
Manufactured in the United States of America.
10 9 8 7 6 5 4 3 2 1   (pbk) 10 9 8 7 6 5 4 3 2 1

Library of Congress Cataloging-in-Publication Data   Kraus, Robert, 1925-   Musical Max / by Robert Kraus;
illustrated by Jose Aruego and Ariane Dewey.   p.   cm.   Summary: The peace and quiet following Max's decision
to put his instruments away drives the neighbors just as crazy as his constant practicing did. [1. Music—
Fiction.]   I. Aruego, Jose, ill.   II. Dewey, Ariane, ill.   III. Title. PZ7.K868Mu   1990[E]—dc20   89-77079
CIP   AC
ISBN: 0-671-68681-X   ISBN: 0-671-79250-4 (pbk)

Max was musical.
You name the instrument
and Max could play it.

trombone

bass

xylophone

flute

Max played by note and Max played by ear.
And Max practiced, practiced, practiced.

small harmonica

cymbals

synthesizer

"Max's practicing is driving me crazy!"
  said Max's father.
"I'm getting tune deaf."
"Practice makes perfect," said Max's mother.
"Here, put on some ear muffs. It will muffle
  the sound."

"It doesn't muffle enough," said Max's father.
"Oh, for a child without talent!"
"From your side, maybe. From my side, impossible,"
said Max's mother.

But it wasn't only Max's father. The whole neighborhood complained.

"We can't stand the noise," they said.
"It's not noise," said Max's mother. "It's music!"
"Call it what you like," they said.
"It's bursting our eardrums."

Max, practicing, was not unaware of the complaints.
But he kept on practicing.
"Music hath charms," he sighed, "but not for them."

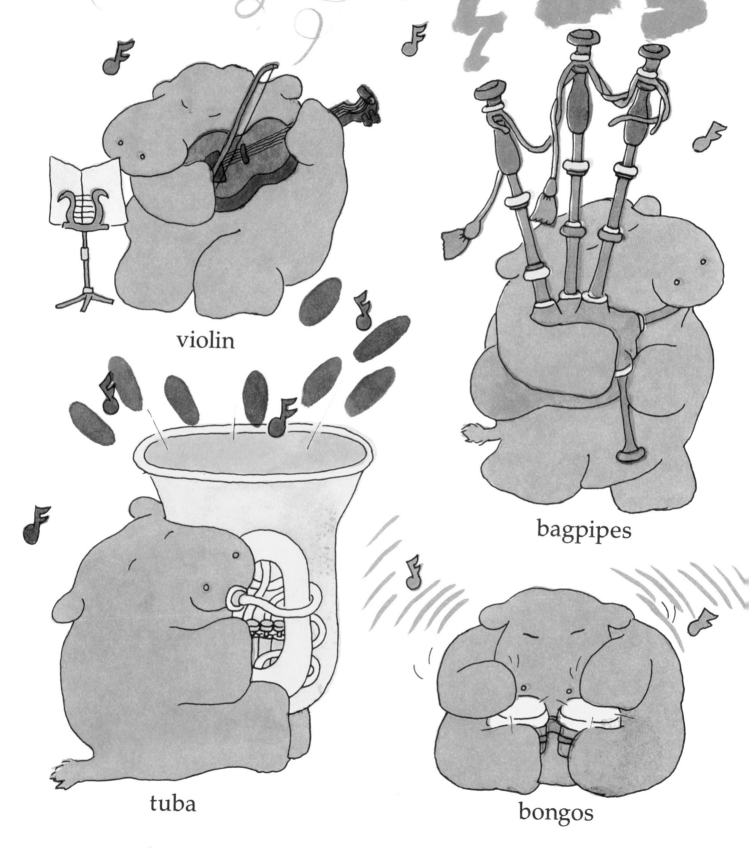

violin

bagpipes

tuba

bongos

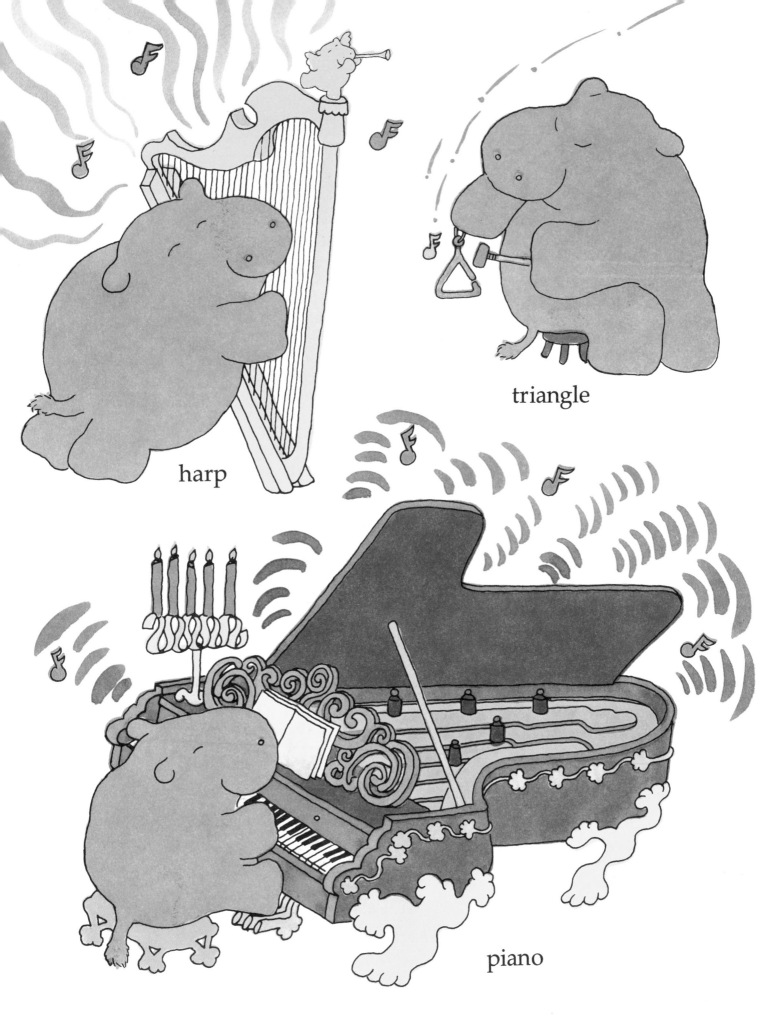

harp

triangle

piano

Only at night was there a little peace and quiet.
Except when Max's father snored.
That was like thunder and lightning.

And except when the whole neighborhood snored.
That was like explosions!

Sometimes the snoring woke Max up.
Then he would begin to practice,
which woke the snorers up.
But it didn't happen too often.
Thank goodness.

But what did happen was that one day
Max stopped playing and practicing.
He put all of his instruments away.

"I'm not in the mood anymore," he said.
And he went out and played baseball with the gang.

At first everyone was relieved.
"The peace and quiet. It's wonderful,"
said the neighborhood.

Max's father took off his earmuffs.
Max's mother was sad, but she was a minority of one.

"When will you play again?" asked Max's mother.
"When I'm in the mood," said Max.
"And who knows when that will be."

It wasn't in the fall.
Max's father complained that the peace
and quiet was driving him crazy.
When would Max get in the mood?

It wasn't in the winter.
The whole neighborhood complained that
the peace and quiet was driving them crazy.
When would Max get in the mood?

In the spring
Max heard a little bird sing...
and Max got in the mood!

Max played,
and Max practiced,
and nobody complained.

In fact, they all joined in!

The end.